CONTENTS

13 Traditional Ghost Stories from
LINCOLNSHIRE

THE LUCY TOWER, LINCOLN CASTLE

Copyright © 2003
The Cædmon Storytellers
Published by East Coast Books

Descend, and touch, and enter; hear
The wish too strong for words to name;
That in this blindness of the frame
My Ghost may feel that thine is near.

In Memorium
Alfred Lord Tennyson.

TOM OTTER

There were nine tongues within one head
The tenth went out to seek the bread
To feed the living within the dead.

MANY YEARS AGO, the Sun Inn at Saxilby was famous for miles around for an old and bloodstained piece of wood with which an itinerant workman had beaten his wife to death. Tom Otter was the man's name, Mary Kirkham, his bride of barely four hours, his victim.

Tom had been forced to marry Mary by the parish authorities, because she was going to have his baby, and had good reason to be rid of her, for he already had a wife in Newark! After the hasty ceremony at St. Mary's Church, they two set off together along the road to Saxilby and Mary was never seen alive again.

A farm worker had seen Tom take his bride down a little lane off the main road, but return alone. Intrigued, the man went to investigate, and found Mary's battered corpse.

Within a week, Tom was arrested and locked in Lincoln Castle. At his trial the bloodstained hedge stake which he had used to kill his wife was produced as evidence and Tom, who until then had pleaded his innocence, broke down and confessed his crime.

The sentence of the court was that Tom should be hanged at Lincoln castle, then his body taken to the site of his crime, there to be GIBBETED: hung in chains as an example to others.

In the days before television, people took an even greater interest in murders than they do now, it is not surprising then, that on the day of the execution a huge crowd gathered to watch Tom hang, then follow the cart which took his body to the gibbet.

So great was the interest in Tom Otter's crime that the landlord of the nearby Sun Inn at Saxilby, an astute man, purchased the hedge stake used in the crime and put it on display. Soon his pub was doing a roaring trade as people came from miles around to look at the gibbet, then view the bloody hedge stake and drink in the bar.

Gradually interest in Tom Otter and his hedge stake faded as more recent crimes began to grab the public's notice. The landlord's fortunes would certainly have suffered had it not been for a ghostly incident which now occurred. On the first anniversary of the murder the landlord suddenly noticed that the hedge stake had disappeared from its shelf. He immediately sent two of the village's most talkative men to the site of the gibbet and there, to their amazement, the stake was found dripping, they said, with fresh blood! Very soon everybody knew about the 'MIRACLE', and the Sun Inn was as busy as ever.

Another year passed, and the Sun Inn was quiet again when the landlord noticed that once again the hedge stake had disappeared! Once more an expedition was sent out to the gibbet, and once again the stake was found at the base in a pool of blood, thus boosting the Sun Inn's waning popularity.

With the approach of the third anniversary, the landlord announced that a watch was to be kept over the hedge stake, and great interest was shown from as far away as Nottingham. On the night, the Sun Inn was packed with drinkers, all keen to keep watch (and drink) all through the night. Much to their disappointment, at eleven o'clock, the landlord announced that the bar was closing, and that only he and a couple of his trusted friends were to stay and keep watch. Lamenting loudly, the drunkards skulked their way home. Next morning, the hedge stake was once more found, blood soaked, by the gibbet. Though none of those watching in the pub would admit to falling asleep.

BY THE FOURTH YEAR, so great was the public interest, that the landlord had great difficulty in closing the Sun Inn, and his pub was surrounded right through the night by hundreds of people hoping to see the ghostly figure of Tom Otter coming to collect his murder weapon. Great was their disappointment the following morning, for the hedge stake had not moved, the ghost obviously deterred by the huge crowd.

After this incident, people began to lose interest in the hedge stake, and the following year the landlord sold the pub and left the district. Tom Otter's gibbet, however, had passed into local folklore. The path on which it stood was even renamed 'TOM OTTER'S LANE', and no-one ever passed that way without going for a look at Tom's rotted corpse, and the birds which had taken to nesting in his skull. Tom and the birds were even immortalized in a local children's nursery rhyme or riddle:

There were nine tongues within one head
The tenth went out to seek the bread
To feed the living within the dead.

Finally, in 1850, the gibbet collapsed and Tom's few remains were buried on the spot. The irons in which he was hung were taken as souvenirs and can be seen at Doddington Hall to this day, while the wood from the gibbet was made into a chair for the local doctor.

As to the fate of the hedge stake, nothing is known. It is just possible, though, that if you go to a certain spot on Tom Otter's Lane in the early morning of November the third you may find it, still gory with dripping, fresh, blood!

1806 March 14, Thomas Tempor Alias Otter For murdering his wife, hung in chains near Drisney Nook.
From "A Correct Account of All The Executions That have taken place at Lincoln, from 1722, to the present time."

BAYARD'S LEAP

NORTH OF THE VILLAGE of Ancaster, by the ancient Roman road of Ermine Street, near the place we now call Byard's leap, lies an old quarry. In the quarry there used to live a witch called Meg. The walls of her decrepit house were the sides of the quarry, her roof was of twisted branches and thatch so old that it was covered in grass and weeds so thick that no one would have known she lived there had it not been for her reputation. For Meg was a wicked witch, and it was said that she could wither a crop of corn, OR CRIPPLE A COW with a single glance from her evil eye.

For hundreds of years the local people had followed the custom of taking offerings of corn, salt and honey every spring and harvest time, and leaving them at a little shrine in front of Meg's hovel to propitiate the witch and guarantee that she would not do any evil deeds against them. For many hundreds of years this had worked. The land was rich and dark, the grass moist and green, the sheep in the fields, healthy and fat.

BUT there came a time when the local vicar opened a school and introduced the young people of the village and the surrounding farms to book learning. Soon the children began to scoff at the idea that an evil witch lurked in the quarry, and the old custom, passed on from father to son since time immemorial, fell into decline. Some of the older, wiser, folks shook their heads and insisted that the witch was there, and though they had to admit that they had never actually seen her, they warned of the dire consequences of failing to honour her shrine. But the young people laughed, and repeated what the vicar told them, that the shrine was no more than a relic from Roman times when travelers left offerings to their pagan gods in hope of a safe journey.

At first they did not notice the changes - a poor harvest here, a sick sheep there. Perhaps a new fence blown down by a freak wind, or a healthy plough horse falling dead in its traces. But slowly they came to realise that what the old folks said was true, as the the farms for miles around Meg's hovel became neglected or abandoned, and the once fertile countryside began to turn into a barren heath.

One spring it was decided that Meg's shrine should be cleaned, and special offerings left for her to bring back good fortunes. The vicar shook his head sadly as he saw the procession setting off to Meg's shrine, lamenting that his people should fall back into their superstitious ways.

But the villagers' plan failed to work, indeed it seemed as if they had angered Meg all the more, for the next week, the richest farmer in the village went broke, and his tools and livestock were taken off by the bailiffs. Even the vicar suffered, for the farmer had six children, and could no longer afford to send them to school.

The people of Ancaster were desperate and, finding that they could not placate Meg, decided on a simple, and effective method of dealing with her: murder. They drew lots to decide who would do the terrible but necessary deed, and the task fell to the local shepherd, a man who was afterwards known as "Brave Jack". The plan the villagers devised was that Jack should tempt the witch out of her lair and murder her. The villagers would then come and bury the body in a secret place.

The shepherd needed a horse, it was decided, for if he went on foot, the witch would have plenty of time to cast spells on him. Every horse in the parish was led down to the village pond and the shepherd invited to take his pick.

He could have had the squire's race horse, Dasher, or the doctors hunter, which could jump over a ten-foot hedge, but Jack was either very sly or a poor horseman, for he decided to choose the most gentle and placid animal he could find. As the horses stood drinking, Jack threw a stone into the middle of the pond, and as the wave spread out, watched what happened. Every horse shied away in fear and surprise, except one. Bayard. Bayard was a plough horse, big, slow and, as it happened, completely blind. This was the horse the shepherd chose.

One thing more was needed. A weapon. Jack himself had a small knife which he carried for cutting pieces of string, but the villagers didn't think it was adequate. The squire offered him a pistol to shoot her, the black smith a great hammer "to beat her brains out." But then, to everyone's surprise, the vicar appeared, carrying the large ancient sword which hung above a knight's tomb in the church. "Take this" he said, and walked, sadly, back to his empty school room.

The largest saddle which they could find was strapped to Bayard's back and Jack, sword in hand, climbed up and set off north along the old Roman road.

Soon Jack was outside Meg's hovel, and he called out: "Come you for a ride, mother - I have the finest steed in Christendom". And she shouted back:

> "I'LL BUCKLE ME SHOES AN' SUCKLE ME CUBS,
> AN' I'LL SOON BE WITH YOU ME LADDIE!"

And out came the witch with great goggling eyes, wild hair, huge teeth and claws.

> "BE OF GOOD CHEER MASTER", she screeched,
> "I WOULD RIDE WITH YOU TO HELL!"

The shepherd had chosen his mount well, for no other horse could have been confronted by such a dreadful sight without turning tail and bolting. But Blind Bayard, blissfully unaware, obeyed the shepherd's command and trotted towards the witch. Jack pulled out the sword, and lunged at the her. But though Meg was very old, she was very agile and, dancing from the blade, leaped over the shepherd's shoulder and landed on Bayard's rump. The great black claws on her feet dug into Bayard's flank and gave it such a fright that Bayard made a single leap of sixty feet, taking off so fast that it left its shoes behind, and landing so hard that its hooves sank deep into the soil. Jack

Page 10

turned and slashed at the witch so hard that he cut her in two, the pieces falling on either side of Blind Bayard. But the sword was so sharp that it went deep into the horse's flesh, and the poor creature bled to death on the spot.

It was a matter of seconds for the shepherd to finish his work, running into the old hag's hovel and stabbing the cubs she was keeping there; little red demons whom she fed on her own blood.

Now that the witch was gone the people thereabouts gradually returned, ploughing the fields again, tending their sheep so that the heath turned once more into rich farmland. But they did not forget that stoic horse.

By the side the road you can still see today four horse shoes placed by the grateful people to mark the spot where Blind Bayard made its giant leap, and on the other side, hidden in the grass, four more to show where that trusty animal landed and, alas, died.

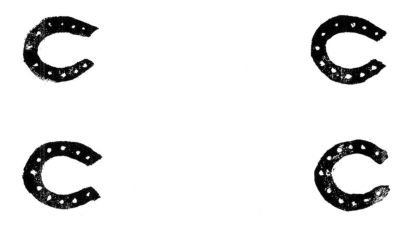

JOHNNY I'THE GRASS

Many years ago there was an old miser who lived near Horncastle, called "Johnny I'the grass". Not only was Johnny I'the grass a miser, he was a "Wiseman" with strange powers. Wonderous tales were told about him after he died; how he once rode a donkey to a toll road, and on being told that the fee was,

"nothing for yourself, as you are a man,
a penny for the donkey because it is not",

that he got off the donkey and muttered a few words in the animal's ear, whereupon the donkey turned into a short and hairy man! How the pair walked past the toll bar, paying nothing, before Johnny whispered into his new companion's ear again and turned it once more into a donkey. Then Johnny climbed onto its back and rode on his way.

THE TIDDY MUN

THE FENS around the Wash were once the home of the Fen Tiger and the Tiddy Mun.

Fen Tigers, or "Slodgers", were the local people, famous for being "all hair and teeth", who lived in the old un-drained marshes.

The Tiddy Mun was a "Wil o' the Wisp", a spirit of those marshes, and it is debatable which was the stranger, for the Fen Tigers were an unusual lot.

Fen Tigers all suffered from "Fen Ague", a form of malaria, which made them fall periodically into dreadful black moods of despair, and their limbs to shake. The symptoms could only partially be controlled by OPIUM, to which they soon became addicted.

Added to this was their dress and mode of living. The Fen Tigers were hunter-gatherers, living in harmony with their habitat. They clothed themselves in animal pelts, otter-skin trousers, trout-skin boots.

Their mode of transport was outlandish, for there were few roads in the old marshes and the twisting, primitive tracks, often disappeared under water when it had rained. So the Fen Tiger either went by Punt; a light, flat bottomed boat which could float over clear water and slide over reed beds, or he took his stilts, which allowed him to follow submerged tracks without getting wet. So skilled were the Fen Tigers at stilt-walking, that many of them used them all the time, never setting foot on the ground unless it was to go into their homes.

The Fen Tiger's diet, was unbalanced, they lived largely on fish and fowl, eating few vegetables and often suffered from scurvy. The men grew great beards to hide the scabs which they often developed as a result of this disease. Some of the women also grew beards, but most hid their blemishes by coating their skin with white face powder. Unfortunately, the powder contained Lead Oxide, which poisoned them and sent them all a little mad.

Since tooth-loss was common amongst the Fen Tigers (an unfortunate side effect of scurvy) any of them who had teeth left, even if they were only a couple of blackened stumps, would show them off proudly, grinning ferociously at anyone who passed by.

Amongst these wild people lived the Tiddy Mun. The Tiddy Mun was rarely seen in person, though from his few reported appearances it is known that he lived in mud holes, was small, very old and with a face like worn leather. The Tiddy Mun wormed his way about under the mud and water of the marshes, a pale light glowing in the air above him. It was said that if you followed this light you might find a good place to fish, or on one particular night of the year only, the secret burial place of lost treasure.

If a Fen Tiger succeeded in following this little light and his hunting was good, he would leave a little present as thanks, perhaps a penny, maybe a grain of opium. Thus the Tiddy Mun was to the Fen Tigers a good spirit with whom they lived in harmony and with MUTUAL RESPECT for hundreds, maybe thousands, of years.

EVENTUALLY, though, things changed. Under the vast marshes which once covered much of Lincolnshire, Norfolk, Cambridge and even South Yorkshire, lay rich, black, soil. In the 17th Century, Dutch engineers were brought over to England to drain and expose this fine agricultural land. The Fen Tigers, of course, opposed this drainage which was destroying their way of life. They did this mainly by legal means, electing Oliver Cromwell (SOMETHING OF A FEN TIGER HIMSELF) to oppose the changes in parliament

The Tiddy Mun, however, found other means to thwart the drainage. Many a Dutch engineer met a lonely and unmarked grave having lost his way home at the end of a day's work. In the twilight he would see what he thought was a lantern waving in the distance, a faint voice beckoning him to safety. But it was the Tiddy Mun, drawing the hapless fellow deeper into the treacherous marshes to a cold, watery death.

Sadly, even the Tiddy Mun and Cromwell combined could not stop the halt the march of progress. Within a hundred years, the marshes, the Fen Tigers and even the Tiddy Mun had slipped into history.

However, with global warming and rising sea levels, perhaps the marshes will return; the Tiddy Mun will once more creep, glowing under the mud, to lead the drug-addled citizens of Spalding, their stilts hastily dusted off, to some fine fishing spot.

AN OLD CURE FOR AGUE.

Not all fenlanders used opium to control ague: some put spiders in a bag round their neck to protect themselves. Others, believing this was the Devil's work, relied on three horseshoes, nailed to their beds, with a mell (hammer) waiting nearby. For, as one old lady said.

"When the old 'un comes to shake me, Yon'll fix him safe as t'church steeple; he weant nivver pass yon". She explained: "It's a chawm. Oi taks the mell I' moy left hand and I taps they shoes an' says:

'Feyther, Son and Holy Ghoast,
I Naale the divil to this poast.
Throice I strikes with holy crook,
Won fur God, an' won fur Wod,
An' won for Lok.'"

THE JUMPERS OF LINCOLNSHIRE

PERHAPS it is something to do with the flatness of the county, the wide overarching skies, the cold winter winds blowing over dreary stubble fields creating a sense of melancholy, but whatever the cause, the people of Lincolnshire are in the habit of going to any high spot that they can find, then throwing themselves from it. And having landed, mangled, it is natural that their ghosts should haunt the place of their death.

Doddington Hall just outside of Lincoln has its own ghostly jumper, a young lady who threw herself from the roof in the eighteenth century to avoid the amorous attentions of the local squire. Her figure is occasionally seen plunging with a scream into the garden below and many people feel a deep sense of unease when they walk beneath the place of her fatal descent. Fortunately, her negative influence is more than balanced by the ghost of an old lady who haunts the first floor landing. Though she is only seen for a second or so, she exudes a sincere feeling of welcome to those visitors who are lucky enough to witness her brief appearances.

Perhaps the most attractive spot from the suicide's point of view is the "Boston Stump", the high tower of St. Botolph's Church, Boston. At least two people jumped from the tower in the nineteenth century, one of whom broke her fall (and her neck) on an unfortunate pedestrian who happened to be passing below. One ghost, who still regularly falls from the stump, has been known of since the seventeenth century. It is said to be the ghost of a young girl called Sarah Preston, who, in remorse for bringing plague into the town, threw herself from the top of the tower in 1585. Her ghost is described as being a vague grey figure, who appears on autumn evenings, topples forwards from the stump, and falls silently almost to the ground before disappearing.

A less dramatic, but equally fatal fall is the cause of a haunting in an old house at Louth. It is said that in the 18th Century a maid, being called downstairs by her master to take away some plates from the dining room, went through the wrong door and found herself, not in the kitchen, but tumbling headfirst down the cellar stairs.

Her ghost is invisible, but her footsteps are still heard, hurrying down one flight of stairs and across the dining room. There is a momentary pause, a scream, then a crashing noise from the cellar below.

BOSTON STUMP

THE FAITHFUL SERVANT

"Well done, thou good and faithful servant. Thou hast been
faithful over a few things; I will make thee ruler over many
things. Enter thou into the joy of thy lord."
Matthew 25 vs 21

WE TEND TO HAVE a rose-tinted idea of criminals from
the past. Images of handsome highway men, holding up stage
coaches with a brace of pistols, robbing the rich merchants, but
generously leaving the poor alone, stealing a kiss, perhaps, from
a beautiful lady before giving her back her treasured brooch and
departing into the night. The truth was very different. Many
people were desperately poor, and would violently rob travelers
for no more than a few pence. And kill them too; for death by
hanging was the punishment for highway robbery in those days,
and criminals often thought it was best not to leave a living
witness behind for, it used to be said, "DEAD MEN CAN'T
SPEAK".

Other thieves, after richer pickings, would form gangs
and assault isolated country houses, stealing valuable silver
dishes, jewellery and money. And these men were often even
more violent and desperate than the 'foot pads' who preyed upon
travelers. It is known that on at least one occasion the owner of a
house was roasted alive over the fire to make him reveal the
hiding place of valuables.

And it was poor Jacob Leadle, a boy only fourteen years
old, a servant at Girsby Hall, who met with such a gang as he
made his way home to his master's stately home on a late
summer's afternoon sometime in the late eighteenth century.
Four thieves had been lying in wait for him at the cross roads only

a mile from the house, and dragged him behind a nearby hedge. The boy called for mercy, offered them what little money he had, but the villains just laughed. One of them, carefully and slowly, sharpened a knife on a small stone, testing the edge occasionally until it was, he said, "Sharp enough to flay the skin". The man placed the glittering blade an inch or so from Jacob's eye, telling him that they planned to rob the hall that night and wanted his help. They knew that the owner and his servants slept with guns and pistols near their beds, just in case they were attacked. They needed the boy to unlock the front door at midnight so that they could sneak in quietly and have the advantage of surprise. The knifeman put down his weapon for a second, and told the terrified child reassuringly, that if he did as they said, they would not kill him. But, he continued, picking up the knife again and pressing the glinting point into the boy's chin, that if he told anyone of their plan, they would come back at some other time, and slice every inch of skin from his body.

Then they let him go, laughing and jeering after him, waving their weapons and the knife in the air as he made his way trembling home. Poor Jacob! He was terrified of what was to happen if he did not warn his master, and just as terrified of what might happen if he did. But as he made his way home, he came to a decision.

While the robbers had promised that they would not harm him if he did as they said, he felt he could not trust them - they might well kill him anyway, as an act of extra wickedness. Whereas, if he revealed the plan, there was a good chance that the villains would all be killed or hanged if caught, and they would no longer be a threat to him. So as soon as he entered the house, Jacob asked to see his master, and told him everything. After dark, one of the other servants took a back way to Horncastle and returned by the same route with the local magistrate and a band of well-armed men, who waited silently in ambush for the robbers.

As midnight approached, four figures crept up the hall's front drive, and on the hour, the front door swang silently open.

The villains entered the house and were caught in a hail musket fire, falling to the ground terribly wounded. Amazingly, none of them died. Not then at least. They were thrown into a cart and carried off to Lincoln Castle, blood dripping onto the bumpy road as they went, agonised groans coming from the men each time the wheels hit a rut.

The four criminals lived long enough to go on trial at the quarter sessions, for the owner of the hall made sure they had the best medical treatment so, he said, he could have the pleasure of seeing them hang. They were found guilty, condemned, hanged, and their bodies returned to the spot where they had assailed poor Jacob. There they were Gibbeted, hung in chains from a gallows, one on each corner of the crossroads.

Jacob, was promoted, and became the special favourite of his master. As a mark of his special esteem, he even presented him with an elegant silver fob-watch, inscribed with the words:

JACOB

WELL DONE, THOU GOOD AND FAITHFUL SERVANT!

ANNO 1784

The timepiece was not of much practical use to Jacob, for he never learned to tell the time, but he occasionally opened the case and looked proudly at the words, which though he could not read he knew said 'Well done, thou good and faithful servant!'

It was a few months after the men were hanged, on a late winter's afternoon, that Jacob's master, kind as ever, gave him an extra holiday, and the boy set off from the hall towards Horncastle to see his mother, promising to return the following morning. The other servants was nervous about him leaving so late, for he would have to pass the gibbeted bodies after sunset: they were a superstitious lot, and would never pass the place except in full daylight. But Jacob laughed at them, saying he was not afraid; that dead men couldn't harm him. No one ever saw him again. Alive.

Grumbling to himself, the peddler trudged wearily along the road. He had spent an uncomfortable night in a barn nearby, but had been disturbed by weird lightning which flashed across the sky along with dreadful 'screating' noises - like howls of pain, wafting in the wind. But at the cross roads, he cheered up a little when he saw four gibbeted bodies swinging slowly to and fro in the breeze: he knew there would be no robbers to attack him hereabouts. But there was a strange odour in the air, and the pedlar following the smell found, behind a hedge, Jacob, dead. *His skin, flayed from his body, lying in a bloody heap besides him.* And lying on the skin the silver, engraved watch.

Who killed Jacob? No one knows. The magistrate, the hall's owner and the local vicar were of the opinion that there had been other members of the gang, hiding, waiting for a signal from their comrades, and that these men had slipped away during the ambush, returning months later to take their revenge on the poor lad. But the superstitious servants did not agree. If living men had killed Jacob, they reasoned, they would have stolen his watch. It could only be the ghosts of the hanged men, come back from Hell to wreak their revenge, for they said, ghosts have no use for a silver timepiece in that place.

Whichever is the truth, no one, not even the vicar, ever passed that spot after nightfall for many, many years.

THE GREEN LADY

"Will you hear a Spanish Lady,
How an English man she woo'd.
Tho' he held her as his captive,
Ever gentle was his mood.
Tho' by birth and parentage of high degree
Much she wept when orders came to set her free."
Old Ballad

PERHAPS THE BEST KNOWN GHOST in Lincolnshire is the "Green Lady" who haunts Thorpe Hall near Louth, drifting over the lawns in her famous green dress, peeping in the windows and alarming anyone who happens to be looking out.
The Green Lady was a passionate Spanish Senõrita, taken prisoner by Sir John Bolle, the Hall's owner during the famous raid on Cadiz in 1596.

WHILE the English say that Sir John was unfailingly polite and courteous to his prisoner, just as they portray the raid on Cadiz as a wise pre-emptive strike to prevent the Spaniards invading England, the Spanish, who regard the English raid as pure piracy and robbery, say he was a love-rat, who seduced the poor woman, keeping it a secret that he had a wife and family at home.

WHICHEVER was the truth, when Sir John Bolle came to release his prisoner, she wanted to return to England with him. After giving her many spurious reasons why she should not do so, such as that his ship might be attacked by a GIANT LOBSTER on the way home, or that the crew were too smelly for a woman of fine breeding to endure, he finally admitted that he was married.

The Spaniards say that the lady fell in a faint and died soon after of a broken heart, and that Sir John Bolle stole all her possessions, going so far as to cut off the corpse's fingers to get at the golden rings. The English, on the other hand say that the woman, knowing that the noble Sir John was the only person she could ever love, but was unattainable, gave him her blessing, and her gold, and joined a nunnery.

IN EITHER CASE, Sir John returned to England very much richer, and with a portrait of the lady in a brilliant green dress, which hung for over a hundred years at the top of the main staircase.

The English version of the story relates that the Spanish Lady soon left the nunnery and followed Sir John to England, believing either that he was not in fact married, or that she could persuade Sir John to leave his wife, but on seeing him happily at home with his young family, hanged herself from an oak tree in the front garden.

WHETHER a broken heart or a broken neck did for the pretty Señorita, we can never know. But for British honour's sake, I am pleased to say that there are two reasons for suspecting that the English version of the tale may be true.

FIRSTLY, the Green Lady is as harmless a ghost as might wish to meet, if you would like to meet one, that is. She Floats silently around the gardens of Thorpe Hall in her beautiful flowing green dress, but does no harm. She might alarm you if she floats through a hedge and appears suddenly, but she has never been known to act with malice, shaking people awake at midnight or screaming or breaking plates.

SECONDLY, Sir John Bolles' reaction to the ghost itself. He never showed any signs of alarm at the ghost's presence, and indeed insisted that a place be set at the dinner table for the green lady in case she decided to pop in, (a tradition continued at the hall to this day), and always had his family toast her health when they drank from his store of **PLUNDERED SPANISH WINE!**

THE HOLBEACH GAMESTERS

THE CHEQUERS INN was once the haunt of four notorious drunkards; Abraham Tegerdine; Dr. Jonathan Watson; Mr. Slater and Farmer Guymer. Every night the four of them would sit in the bar drinking and gambling, and were so well known, that they even had their own bench. And they had sat on it for so long, that there were four depressions in it the shape of their **BOTTOMS**.

All their late nights and drinking eventually undermined Farmer Guymer's health, and after a short illness, he died. The three survivors decided to hold a wake for their departed friend in the Chequers the night before the funeral, but found to their dismay that now that there were only three of them, and they were not squashed together, their bottoms expanded beyond the depressions which they had worn in the bench. No matter what they did, **WRIGGLING ABOUT** and swapping places, they could not get comfortable. There was nothing to do, they decided, but to get old Farmer Guymer out of his coffin and back into his own seat. The landlord, however, refused to have the body in his pub (not out of squeamishness, but on principal - he would not allow anyone to sit in the bar all night without spending a penny), so the three men picked up their bench and carried it over to the church, where their friend lay, **COLD AND SILENT**, in his coffin.

In a few moments the corpse was popped into its old place, a tankard of ale pressed into its lifeless hand and a pipe into its mouth. The three old drunkards even dealt out cards to their friend, taking turns at playing for him. Strangely enough, the dead man won nearly every hand. But the three living were not too concerned about the success of the dead. "Why" said Dr. Watson, "we'll share his money out again at the end of the night! He doesn't need it where he's gone!" And so the friends began to play wildly and with bigger stakes.

IT WAS JUST STRIKING MIDNIGHT when the card game came to an end, the three men's pockets were empty, every penny piled in front of Farmer Guymer's corpse. "Please Can we have our money back?" Said Dr. Watson, taking off his hat and bowing mockingly towards the dead man - which opened up its eyes, pulled the pipe from its mouth and leered menacingly at the three astonished friends. Slowly, it raised its bloodless arm to point over their shoulders to the figures of three ghastly demons who were waiting to carry them off to Hell.

The following morning the cards, the bench and Guymer's corpse were found, but of the three friends nothing more was ever seen. EXCEPT THAT..... ever since that time drunkards from the town of Holbeach (AND THERE ARE MANY OF THEM), while staggering past the church in the early hours of the morning, report that they have seen three shadowy figures swaying in the porch. These ghostly shapes beckon them, holding up tankards of ale tempting them towards the church, luring them, perhaps, towards a certain doom.

THE GHOSTLY DOG

IN THE GROUNDS OF LINCOLN CASTLE, atop the Lucy tower is a small gravestone, identical in shape to the ones around it, marked simply WC 1877. Beneath it lies the body of William Clark, the last man to be hanged at the castle.

William Clark was a poacher, a bully and an all round bad sort, who always carried with him a stout stick to beat anyone who annoyed him. He was the leader of a gang of ruffians who obeyed him not through love or loyalty, but through fear and loathing - fear of his vile temper and loathing of his vicious stick.

Wherever Clark went, there followed a few paces behind him his FAITHFUL DOG, a Skinny Lurcher. It had often felt the weight of Clark's stick, and its back was scarred and bent from the beatings. Clark and his dog could often be found (if anyone wanted to find them) in the bar of the Strugglers Inn, in the shadow of the castle walls. The lean dog would squeeze itself under a chair or skulk in a tight corner gazing nervously at its master, while Clark would lean on the bar, elbows spread, clearing a great space around him. If ever Clark's eye fell on the terrified dog, it would wag its tail frantically and yelp in a most pathetic manner, a mixture of fear and hope - fear that Clark had taken it into his mind to beat the animal, as he often did, and hope that he might for once show some affection to the faithful animal: for In the whole town this poor mistreated dog was the only living creature which cared a jot whether Clark lived or died.

One evening, as Clark was drinking in the bar of the Strugglers, he noticed that it had gone strangely quiet. Turning round, he was confronted by two constables who had come to arrest him over the death of a gamekeeper. Clark pulled out his trusty stick, but it was to no avail, for the constables in their turn pulled out truncheons and after a short and vicious struggle Clark was carried, bloody and unconscious, to the gaol within the prison.

Clark was indicted for murder; he had shot a game keeper while out poaching with his gang and the man, after seeming to recover for a few days, had developed gangrene. The surgeons lopped off limb after limb in an attempt to save him, but he eventually died in dreadful pain a month or so later.

After Clark's arrest his gang, fearing for their safety, turned what was known as "QUEEN'S EVIDENCE" so that, after making full confessions laying the majority of the blame on Clark, they were not prosecuted for their part in the crime.

Against the confessions of his gang, Clark could make no defence. He was found guilty of murder, and sentenced to death.

Clark's dog now had nowhere to go, and would skulk around the walls of the castle, looking forlornly for its master. Sometimes it would scratch around the door of the Strugglers Inn and stare into the bar expecting, perhaps, to find him there. But the landlord chased it away, for it reminded his customers of the loathsome villain Clark and could not be tolerated. Indeed it would have starved, had it not been for the kindness of the landlord's wife, who gave it the odd scrap of gristle or stale bread, hiding her kind act by throwing it at the animal's head and shouting "And I hope it chokes you!"

Even though PUBLIC EXECUTIONS had long ago been abandoned, people would still gather on the morning of an execution. They would congregate first in Castle Square to watch the hangman come from his lodgings carrying, as he always did, the little black bag which contained the prisoner's shackles and the noose. Then they would go to the strugglers Inn, drinking and laughing on the street outside. For here in times past it had been possible to see the hanging itself. Pie-sellers and Chapmen selling copies of the condemned man's "LAST CONFESSION" would do a roaring trade until a few minutes before 7 o'clock. For then a nervous silence would fall over the crowd as they imagined the scene inside the prison: the hangman entering the condemned cell, shackling the man's hands behind him, the grim procession to the new drop, the priest chanting prayers at the front, the hangman adjusting the noose at the back. And then the final moments, the hood over the head, the lever pulled, the fall, the snapping of neck bones and the creaking of the gallows as the corpse swung slowly to and fro.

The people outside were, of course, generally ignorant of the actual moment of death, but traditionally took the chiming of the cathedral clock as a sign that the deed was done. But that day they all knew the exact moment when the felon died. For suddenly Clark's dog, which had been sniffing around the crowd begging for scraps, began to **WHIMPER DREADFULLY**, its body rigid in fear, staring at the castle as if it could see through the walls - could see its master, his hands bound, stumbling, tremblingly towards the gallows. At a few minutes before seven the dog suddenly went rigid, tilted back its head, and let out such a mournful howl that it chilled the blood of every soul that heard it. There was no doubt in anyone's mind that it was this, and not the striking of the clock, which marked the moment that Clark had been launched into eternity.

After this eerie incident, Clark's dog became a veritable celebrity in the Bailgate and was now as welcome in the Strugglers as it had been reviled before. People would come from miles around to see "CLARK'S AMAZING DOG". The animal itself did not enjoy its new elevated status, however, for it looked even more miserable now that its master had gone, and grew even thinner than before despite the landlord offering it the choicest morsels to tempt its appetite, and the wife continuing to throw rotten scraps at its head and shout "I hope it chokes you". Eventually the poor animal died, but the landlord, not wishing to loose such an attraction, had it stuffed and displayed behind the bar for for many years.

The spirit of the dog could not rest, and it haunted the walls of the castle for many years. Sometimes it returned to the Strugglers Inn at midnight, and the Landlord and Landlady would lie terrified in their beds as they heard the SCRATCHING AND WHINING of the ghostly dog at their front door.

MANY YEARS PASSED, the landlord and landlady had long gone, even the story of Clark and his amazing dog had faded from the memory of Lincoln folk. Occasionally there was a scratching sound at midnight, but the new landlord of the Strugglers Inn paid no attention to it, thinking it was probably rats. And the "Old Stuffed Dog" in the bar, dusty and decayed now, one glass eye missing, was thrown away.

Yet occasionally, on dark and stormy nights, late revelers still see the figure of that skinny dog lurking beneath the castle walls. It tilts back its head and opens its mouth and lets out such a dreadful, mournful, howl that it chills the blood of the drunkard, filling his heart with such dread that he goes home a sober, sadder man.

THE
MARKBY CHURCH GHOST

MIDNIGHT, and all is quiet as two lads make their way silently towards the door of Markby Church, hammer and nails in their hands, their hearts beating wildly. If all goes well, in a few minutes, they will see THE GHOST!

Markby is a little village in the Lincolnshire Wolds, the church is a pretty building with an old fashioned thatched roof. For hundreds of years there has been a belief that if you run anti-clockwise three times round the church, then hammer a nail into its front door, a ghost will appear. Countless nail-holes show that many people have tried to see this spirit.

The boys near the church, shaking with fear. BOTH WANT TO GIVE UP, but neither dares to admit to the other that they are afraid. Shaking, they approach the door. An owl hoots. The boy's knees knock.

"Ready?" gasps one. The other, afraid that his voice will crack, does not reply, but nods nervously. And off they set, trotting anti-clockwise round the church. One boy, glancing back, is sure he has seen the Devil, and screams. Now they sprint, too afraid to look back.

"Boys again," mutters the vicar, frowning and getting out of bed, his LONG-WHITE NIGHTSHIRT flapping round his legs, "I'm not having this." He puts on his slippers then walks down the stairs and begins to unlatch the vicarage door.

The boys, now gasping for breath, are at the church door, trying to hammer in the nail.

Bang!

"Ouch!" One boy has caught his thumb.

Bang!

"Oy!" Shouts the vicar.

The boys jump at the noise and, turning, see a long gowned figure, glowing in the moonlight, drifting towards them. Screaming, terrified by the sight of the "ghost", they flee, running all the way home, each promising himself that if he lives, he will never go near that place again.

The next day, with the sun shining and birds singing, the horrors of the night before fade away. In the playground, they tell an open-mouthed crowd about their adventure. Boast how brave they were. How the Devil popped out from behind a gravestone and tried to grab them. How the ghost chased them, grimly white, floating over the ground!

And their younger playmates gaze admiringly at these heroes, determined that when they are big, they too will summon up the courage to go, hammer and nail in hand, to raise the Markby Church Ghost.

The Sunken Church
of Dragonby

The law locks up the man or woman
Who steals the geese from off the common:
But lets the greater villain loose
Who steals the common from the goose.
Anon

IN A FIELD, just outside Scunthorpe, there is a long line of stone peeping from the grass. The few courageous people who dare gather by this stone on a certain moonlit night in autumn hear, from deep under the ground, the weird sound of voices singing slow and mournful harvest hymns. The stone is said to be the very top of the church of Dragonby: the voices, those of the accursed inhabitants of that ancient village.

DRAGONBY was once a pretty place. It had a little pond beside the ale house; a few little shops; the blacksmith and the baker; all the things necessary for the honest hardworking inhabitants. It was a happy village too. The farmers ploughed their fields or gathered their crops according to the season, and whistled merrily as they made their way home in the dusk. The old folks tended the roses which grew around their doors, smiling, and gossiping with their neighbours.

The pride of the village was the common, several hundred acres of land which belonged to everyone. Here villagers could keep a few geese and a goat or cow and,on four days of the year, gather firewood. When Sunday came, the young folk went to the common to fly kites or to woo their sweethearts:the old folks to walk and reminisce.

The soil of the common was dark and rich and occasionally the farmers would gather a handful of this soil and imagine how good it would be to plough it up and grow turnips. The villagers,though, loved the common too much to allow anyone to change it. Until one of the farmers, a bit more determined than his neighbours, decided to take matters into his own hands. One spring morning, he took his horse and plough to the common, and there turned over a patch of land. A few people soon gathered, angry that he should do such a thing, but the farmer had his argument ready. He knew how big the common was, and how many people lived in the village, so he had ploughed that fraction of the common which he felt he was entitled to. Why, he said, if they all did the same as him, everyone would have a good-sized piece of land on which they could grow crops and become rich.

A few other farmers, impressed with his logic, immediately went to get their ploughs and, despite the protests of others, began to measure and cultivate "their" patches of land.

Many people in the village did not want the common divided in this way but others, frightened that they were missing out on something, made deals with the farmers who were ploughing, renting them "their field". To mark the different plots, people began to put up fences on the common. As the fencing began, so did the arguments. Some people said every person should get an equal share of the land, others, that each house should have its own plot. Some said their plot should be bigger because the soil was a little thinner than their neighbour's, Others demanded their boundaries should be moved so that they could get access to the pretty little stream which gurgled through the common. And drain it.

Eventually, the arguments became so bad that two lawyers were called in to sort out the legal complexities of dividing common land, and these men, seeing so much needed to be done, bought large houses in the village for themselves.

If the farmers had expected the lawyers would solve all their problems, they soon discovered their mistake. Arguments and disagreements multiplied, and the lawyers, ever more busy, got richer and richer by the arguments.

The old people, who had little money, could not pay to go to law to settle disputes, and soon they were left with nothing, their portion of the common was gobbled up by their more avaricious neighbours

Others too lost out. Some people had to sell their plots because they could not get to them without trespassing on other people's land and trespass, according to the lawyers, was a wicked crime, and should not be allowed. Some of the smaller farmers built up such large debts with the lawyers that they had to sell not only their plot on their common, but their whole farm as well!

The village had changed beyond recognition. Many of the poorer people had gone, forced to leave the village or face cold and starvation that winter: for the common had been their lifeline. However poor they might be, they'd never gone short of firewood, and always had eggs or cheese to go on their plain bread. Those who remained were so worried about money that they no longer whistled merrily on their way home or visited the ale house on the green.

When the harvest was in, there was, as usual, a harvest festival service in the church. But it was very different from the ones which had gone before. The congregation had shrunk, the lawyers and bankers were sitting in the front pews, where in times past gifts of food and clothing had been placed for the needy of the parish. When the vicar came in, they all began to sing a hymn of thanks for the harvest.

THERE IS NOTHING THE DEVIL LOVES MORE than to listen to a crowd hypocrites singing hymns, so he was immediately attracted to the church and sat himself on the roof to enjoy this sweetest of all sounds. His imps began to join him, and they even joined in the choruses!

Perhaps because it was evening, the people in the church did not notice the effect the Devil and his imps were having on the church - their combined weight causing the building to sink slowly into the ground. So the service went on, and the church continued to sink until only the very tip of the roof could be seen poking through the soil.

When the service was finished, the vicar threw open the door. But instead of a moonlit night there was a dark tunnel awaiting which led deep into the infernal parts of the earth - and the Devil with his demons waiting there with sharpened pitchforks.

Once a year, it is said, the Devil allows the people of Dragonby out of Hell to visit the church and sing harvest songs once more, before returning to their torments. Up above, the weird mournful sound of their singing drifts though the autumn air to those who wait in the moonlight. Few have the stomach to stay for long, however, for after half an hour or so, the singing is replaced by agonised groans as the demons herd the villagers from the church. A terrific clang as the doors close, then silence for another year.

JOHNNY I'THE GRASS

MANY YEARS AGO there was an old miser who lived near Horncastle, called "Johnny I'the grass". Not only was Johnny i'the grass a miser, he was a "Wiseman" with strange powers. Wondrous tales were told about him after he died: **HOW** he stopped for a pint of beer in an ale house, and once he had supped made a tree grow out of the pewter mug so high that it went through the roof: **HOW** everyone stood amazed as two dwarfs also popped out of the mug and cut down the tree so that it fell ripping a huge hole in the wall; and **HOW** three birds flew in through the hole, sat down on the table, and pulled off their own heads, then flew around the room, while their heads, still lying on the table, whistling popular tunes, how the birds landed, put their heads back on, and flew back out of the hole in the wall, which disappeared after them, along with the tree and the dwarfs.....**AND** Johnny I'the grass who had not yet paid for his beer!

THE HUNTSMAN
AND THE HARE

GRANNY MARSHALL never went short of a sixpence, for if she ever needed money she would send her little grandson off to the huntsman to tell him she had seen a hare. The huntsman always gave the boy sixpence for this information, and always found a hare to chase too: for while the boy was gone, Granny Marshall turned into a large hare and lolloped off to the spot she had told her grandson, and got ready for the chase.

This hare was the fastest animal in the Lincolnshire Wolds and a hound could never get near it, but for many years it gave the huntsman and his friends a wonderful afternoon of sport for a sixpence. The hare became so famous that people would come from miles around and bring their best hounds to try and catch it.

Then one day the huntsman became suspicious. He had noticed that the hare always turned towards Granny Marshall's house after an hour or so, and when it neared her little cottage, it always managed to disappear. He began to suspect that "The Devil was in the dance": he knew all about witches and their power to turn themselves into hares and rightly suspected that this was what Granny Marshall was doing.

So the next time the little boy came to tell him he had seen a hare, the huntsman set a trap. While some of his friends set off to seek the hare, he went with his best dog and hid in a spot near old Granny Marshall's cottage. After a couple of hours, he heard the sound of baying dogs approaching, and then the hare appeared. The huntsman let loose his hound and it, being fresh, was soon upon the tired hare. The grandson, looking out of the cottage window and, seeing the hound closing on the hare, shouted as loud as he could "Run Granny!", giving her warning.

Just in time she leaped over a thick briar hedge and into an old narrow sunken lane.

The huntsman had heard the boy shouting, and was determined that this time the witch would not escape - he jumped over the same hedge and barred her way.

"Now I've got you" shouted the huntsman.

But the hare did not stop, it ran on towards the huntsman, and with each step, grew bigger. In a few strides, it was as large as a cart horse, and the huntsman only just had time to let out a terrified scream and dive head first into the thorny hedge before the hare thundered past.

As the huntsman picked himself from the hedge, sore and bleeding, he was sure he could hear Granny Marshall's mocking laughter behind him.

A few minutes later his friends and their dogs arrived, and for a moment the huntsman considered going round to Granny Marshall's house and accusing her of witchcraft. But then he thought it would end his sport forever, and kept his peace.

And so it was that Granny Marshall got her sixpences, and the huntsman his sport, with no crafty ambushes, for many, many years.

THE GHOST OF
BOLINGBROKE CASTLE

BOLINGBROKE CASTLE was the birthplace of Henry
Bolingbroke: King Henry the Fourth. Today only a few stones
remain standing of what was once a magnificent fortress. For
several centuries, it was the administrative centre of the Dutchy
of Lancaster, where the family's accounts were checked
annually. The castle was a royalist fortress in the civil war, and
was partly demolished afterwards by Parliament to prevent it
being used again.

The Bodlean Library in Oxford contains a manuscript
dated from the 1650's written by a civil servant sent to check that
no repairs had been carried out.

'One thing is not to be passed by and is affirmed as a certain
truth by many of ye Inhabitants of ye Towne upon their own
Knowledge, which is, that ye Castle is Haunted by a certain
spirit in the Likeness of a Hare which at ye meeting of ye
Auditors doeth usually runne between their legs and
sometymes overthrows them and so passes away. They have
pursued it down into ye Castle yard and seene it take in at a
grate into a low Cellar and have followed it thither with alight,
where notwithstanding that they did most narrowly observe it
(and that there was noe other passage out, but by ye doore, or
windowe, ye room being all framed of stones within, not
having ye least Chinke or Crevice), yet they could never find
it. And at other tymes it hath beene seene run in at the Iron-
Grates below into other of ye Grottos (as thir be many of
them), and they have watched the place and sent for Houndes
and put in after it but after awhile they have come crying out.'

Page 40

THE FARMER
AND THE BOGGART

THERE WAS ONCE a clever farmer who bought a field on a hill near Alford. He had only just gone to walk over the land when he discovered why he had managed to buy it so cheap, for a nasty Boggart lived under the hill and popped out of a little hole near the top, and told the farmer to clear off. But the farmer wouldn't go away. Instead he planted all sorts of crops in the field to see which grew best, carrots and cabbages, broccoli and beans. But the Boggart spoiled everything he planted, CREEPING under the ground and spoiling the roots, or CLOMPING over the land, crushing the young shoots with his great hairy feet. When he found his crops had all failed, the farmer decided to go and see the Boggart and talk things over with him.

"Now this is doing neither of us any good," said the farmer, "Let us come to some agreement. Let us share the crops: you can have everything that grows above the ground, and I will be content with everything that grows beneath."

Well the Boggart was DELIGHTED with this arrangement, and agreed outright, not knowing what a crafty fellow the farmer was. For that year he planted a huge crop of potatoes, so that at the end of the year here was the farmer with a big clamp of juicy potatoes, and there was the Boggart with a heap of old LEAVES AND HAULMS. The Boggart was furious!

"Next year", he screeched, "we'll share the crop again, but this time, I'll have everything which grows under the ground, and you must be content with everything which grows above."

BUT next year, the farmer grew a huge crop of wheat, so that come harvest here was the farmer with a huge stack of wheat, and there was the Boggart, with a pile of old roots.

"Next year," screamed the Boggart, "you won't fool me. We'll share the crop by harvesting it together. What you cut, you shall keep, what I cut shall be mine."

And now the farmer was worried, because a Boggart can cut as much corn in an hour as a man can cut in a long day. Desperate for help, the farmer went to visit a Wiseman, Johnny i'the Grass, who told him to lay bits of iron on the ground where the Boggart was to work, so that his **SCYTHE** would be blunted. So the farmer gathered all the old iron junk he could find and sowed it at the top of the hill near the Boggart's hole, and on the day of the harvest, he went into the middle of the field and called to the Boggart.

"Today is the day for harvest, Boggart, let us begin." Well the Boggart rushed off to his hole to fetch his scythe, while the farmer rushed down to the bottom of the hill and began to cut his corn so that the Boggart would have to start at the top of the hill where the iron was laid.

And after the harvest, here was the farmer with his stack of corn, laughing out loud, and there was the Boggart, cursing, sharpening his scythe, hardly a stoop of corn cut. Boggarts, being sensitive souls, cannot bear to be laughed at. And this one dived down his hole, and sulked so badly that he has never been seen since.

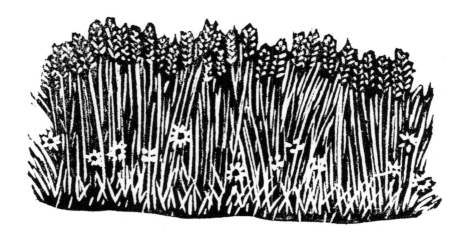

MOTHER NIGHTSHADE
OF GEDNEY

Ay me! for aught that I could ever read,
Could ever hear by tale or history,
The course of true love never did run smooth
Shakespeare.
A Midsummer's Night Dream.

NO ONE ever went by Old Mother Nightshade's cottage after dark for,it was said,she was a witch, and if anyone did, they would return home deranged, mad.....if they returned at all.

But one man summoned up the courage to visit Mother Nightshade: John Culpepper. John Culpepper had fallen madly in love with Rose Taylor, the prettiest girl in the town, but was having little luck in wooing her. He found any excuse to pass her house in the evening but,if he ever met her, he found he was too afraid to speak to her. So he would walk straight on, muttering curses at himself for his shyness. This had the opposite effect on Rose to that which John would have liked, for his lurking about and muttering made her think he was a little simple in the head.

It was in the week before the village fair that John decided he must screw up his courage and approach Rose, for the fair was a famous place for courting and he feared some other lad might woo her there. He waited one morning under a pretty blossoming tree, as romantic a spot as he could imagine, and when Rose came past he greeted her, saying how pretty she looked. With a gallant action, he reached to plucked a bunch of pretty pink blossom for her. Unfortunately, it had been a cold night, and the tree was heavy with dew. As John tugged at the flowers, he sent down a torrent of water onto Rose's head.

"You idiot!" she cried, and went on, dripping wet.

As if this was not bad enough, the following week at the fair Rose pointed him out to her friends, and told her about their meeting, and they all laughed. Humiliated, John went home, on the verge of tears.

So it was the following evening that John made his way apprehensively to old Mother Nightshade's cottage. He crept up the path, and knocked on the door, half expecting that she would come out and scream at him, for she had a dreadful reputation in the village. He was rather surprised when she answered the door and invited him her house, bidding him sit down and make himself comfortable, while she brewed some tea. She was, she said, lonely on a night and always welcomed company. She asked John to tell her about his problems and, cup of tea in hand, he began his story. He told her about his feelings for Rose Taylor, how he had tried to put himself in a position to see her, but was too shy to talk. How their meeting had gone so disastrously wrong, and how she had mocked him at the fair. And he told her how his feelings had changed, how he wanted....Revenge.

Old Mother Nightshade smiled at John, saying she had the very thing and pressing into his hand a little wooden box, sealed with a red ribbon, told him to give it to her on her birthday, not directly, but in a way that she would be sure find out that it was from him.

Now it happened that Rose's birthday fell three days after John's visit to the witch, and on the day, John walked through the town with the box in his hands taking great care to greet everyone he passed and make sure they noticed what he was carrying. He made his way to Rose's house, allowing the gate to slam as he went up the garden, and left the box, with a little posy of blossom, on the doorstep. Then he walked back up the path, noisily kicking the gravel before him, and slammed the gate again. Confident that the girl must surely find out who had given her the box.

Rose was **DELIGHTED** by the box, for it as filled with the most **DELICIOUS CHOCOLATES** she had ever tasted. A few inquiries soon revealed to her who had sent them. Rose looked at the well-made box, the pretty red ribbon and, as she chewed thoughtfully on a delicious chocolate, she smiled.

The next day as John was walking down the road, what did he see, but Rose, standing under the same blossom tree where they had met a week or so before. She was waiting for him! Rose smiled warmly at John, hoping he would stop to court her, but he didn't stop, he kept on walking, and though he smiled back at her, it was a smile of triumph. Rose made her way home again, puzzled.

That evening John returned to old Mother Nightshade's cottage, and told her that he was sure that Rose knew that he had sent her the box, and how she had waited for him, hoping that he would talk to her! His eyes gleamed **MALICIOUSLY** as he asked what was to happen next, how was his **REVENGE** on the girl to come about.

The old woman said nothing for a few minutes, peering at the young man, shaking her head. Finally she told him that she would reveal the revenge to him if he wanted, but he must do exactly as she said. She took from her cupboard a length of rope and tied John's hands to the arms of the chair, saying it was necessary, then bound his feet the same. In the growing gloom she lit two candles and placed them on the mantle piece. Then she turned to John, her eyes flaming with anger.

"**YOU FOOL!**" she screamed, "Did you think I would help you to harm that young maid? I was once like her, young, pretty: ill-treated by an oaf like you.

"I gave you the chance to woo her, fair and square, I gave you some chocolates for her, but you just want revenge for your hurt feelings! Well now I will dispose of your future forever!"

And slowly as poor John watched, Old Mother Nightshade turned into a slavering sharp-fanged wolf.

All through the night the people of Gedney heard dreadful howls and groans from Old Mother Nightshade's cottage, but no one dared to investigate. Instead they double locked the doors and pulled their bedclothes tightly round their ears.

In the morning a few brave souls went to the cottage and found inside the mangled remains of John Culpepper, bitten and torn by sharp teeth. And all around the floor were the bloody paw prints of a wolf. The vicar, of course did not believe any of the tales he was told him about Mother Nightshade and her "Shape Twisting", and John was buried quietly without fuss. But the villagers knew, for they burned down her cottage, and would not even walk over the land where it had stood for many many years.

Mother Nightshade was never seen again - at least not in Gedney. As for Rose, she married a young farmer later in the same year, and he, perhaps wisely, treated her very, very well and they lived happy ever after.

JOHNNY I'THE GRASS
AND THE DEVIL

MANY YEARS AGO there was an old miser who lived near Horncastle, called "Johnny i'the grass". Not only was Johnny i'the grass a miser, he was a "Wiseman" with strange powers. Wonderous tales were told about him after he died; How he got his powers by going into a grave yard on St. Mark's eve with three pewter plates and holding them under a gorse bush to catch the tiny seeds which fell at midnight. How these were the Devil's own seeds, so tiny and heavy that they fell through two of the three pewter plates he held beneath them, and almost knocked Johnny to the ground. How Johnny whistled once, how the Devil appeared, riding his donkey to buy them, how they argued for hours over the price, and how they parted happily as dawn was breaking, both thinking that they had swindled the other!

"OLD JEFFREY", THE EPWORTH PHENOMEN

You might think that no sensible person would take ghosts seriously. And only persons who were **SLIGHTLY DERANGED** would go to the extent of investigating ghosts or writing books about them. You might be right.

However, if this is so, we are not only ones.

John Wesley, who founded the Methodist Church was a great believer in ghosts, and wrote in his diary: "With my latest breath I will bear testimony (to the) one great proof of the invisible world; I mean that of witchcraft and apparitions, confirmed by the testimony of all ages."

John Wesley had very good reasons to believe in ghosts. While he was away at school, his father, the Reverend Samuel Wesley, preached an angry sermon to the people in his parish of Epworth over their foolishness superstitions, their fear of ghosts, and their habit of consulting "**CUNNING-FELLOWS**" who they believed could protect them from the attacks of witches.

Within a week a ghost had moved into the Wesley's rectory, throwing furniture around the place, groaning hideously and terrifying the servants by appearing unexpectedly as "a headless badger".

The Reverend Samuel Wesley at first refused to acknowledge the existence of the ghost, and said it was caused by rats behind the wall. He employed a Scotsman to play his bagpipes in the house, believing this would surely drive the rats away. Instead of this, however "Old Jeffrey" as the children had come to call him, learned to imitate the sound, adding this to the torments which the family had to endure.

Samuel took more drastic steps when the ghost began to rattle the windows whenever he said grace at meal times. Still convinced that the noise was that of rats, he purchased a vicious Bull Mastiff dog. Unfortunately, the dog, unlike its master, believed in ghosts, and was so terrified that it would "tremble and creep away before the noises began."

Unable to ignore the ghost anymore, Wesley invited it to his study for a conference. The ghost pushed the vicar roughly around the room, and made strange noises, but did not afterwards interfere with the family's prayers. The children had actually become fond of Jeffrey and included him in their games, rapping on the walls, and getting him to reply. Then on January the first, 1717, Old Jeffrey disappeared as suddenly as he had appeared a month earlier. Much to the disgust of the young John Wesley who, being a boarder at Westminster school, had missed the entire exciting episode.

Wesley, his imagination fired by the incidents, saved all the letters his family sent him, and on returning home, took statements from the servants. He became so convinced that the ghost was genuine that he had an article on the subject printed in The Arminian Magazine. Great national interest was shown in what was soon known as "The Epworth Phenomenon". A legal expert called doctor Fitchett on reading Wesley's account, went as far as to say: "the evidence, if it were given in a court of law, and in a trial for murder, would suffice to hang any man."

But what of Old Jeffrey? Although he moved out of the Rectory, he would still pop back occasionally to rattle the dinner plates and howl in the night. During one of these visits, the spirit took a shine to John Wesley himself, and although he still visited other members of the family (his sister Emily wrote in February 1750, "that wonderful thing called by us Jeffrey, how certainly it calls on me against any extraordinary new affliction"), he attached himself to this famous preacher for the rest of his life, following him around wherever he went. On one occasion, Old

Jeffrey even brought his friends along. Wesley was staying in a house just outside of Boston, where he was to preach the following day. At midnight he was woken by the sound of laughter, and on coming downstairs found Jeffrey, the Devil, and several demons sitting at the kitchen table with a lovely feast before them. The Devil offered Wesley a seat, but he wisely refused, muttering a few prayers and going back to bed.

Finally, when Wesley died, Old Jeffrey sought out one of the preacher's favourite spots, and settled down in a Methodist Chapel in Whitby, North Yorkshire, for Wesley wrote in his journal "in all England, I have not seen a more affectionate people than those of Whitby." Jeffrey, known locally as "The Whispering Ghost", haunted this chapel for many years, and his activities there are recorded in "**13 GHOST STORIES FROM WHITBY**" Available from the Cædmon Storytellers!

THE END

Also by
The Cædmon Storytellers

13 GHOST STORIES FROM WHITBY Based on the folklore of this quaint seaside town, it was the Cædmon Storytellers first book and is still turning hairs grey! More ghosts and ghouls than you can shake a stick at. But beware, some of these ghosts don't take very well to people shaking sticks at them!

THE WITCHES OF NORTH YORKSHIRE A chance to meet the notorious witches of North Yorkshire. All of these women actually lived, but whether they could really cast spells or fly about on broomsticks we cannot say. What is important though, is that their neighbours believed they could, and the tales of their antics, passed down through the generations are still with us today.

THE HAUNTED COAST Following the Phenomenal success of 13 Ghost Stories from Whitby, the Cædmon Storytellers continued their research along the whole length of the Yorkshire coast, leaving no dank and eerie crypt unexplored, visiting (and drinking in) every haunted pub they could find to bring you The Haunted Coast, thirteen of the best Traditional Ghost Stories from the Humber to the Tees.

THE GHOSTS AND GHOULS OF THE EAST RIDING How do they do it? *Why do they do it?* The Caedmon Storytellers have braved the sound of screaming skulls in haunted houses, dodged wicked witches in their flea-infested hovels and waited for the midnight hour in many a wayside inn where, amazingly, pint after pint of foaming beer disappeared before their very eyes!

The caedmon Storytellers, still drenched in sweat and shaking, bring you **13 TRADITIONAL GHOST STORIES FROM NORFOLK** - a county dripping with gore and ghosts.

Eyes wide with terror, the Caedmon Storytellers have survived, but only just, to bring you **THE GHOSTS AND GHOULS OF YORK**, the world's most haunted city. Read it if you dare...

Printed in Great Britain
by Amazon

36149256R00030